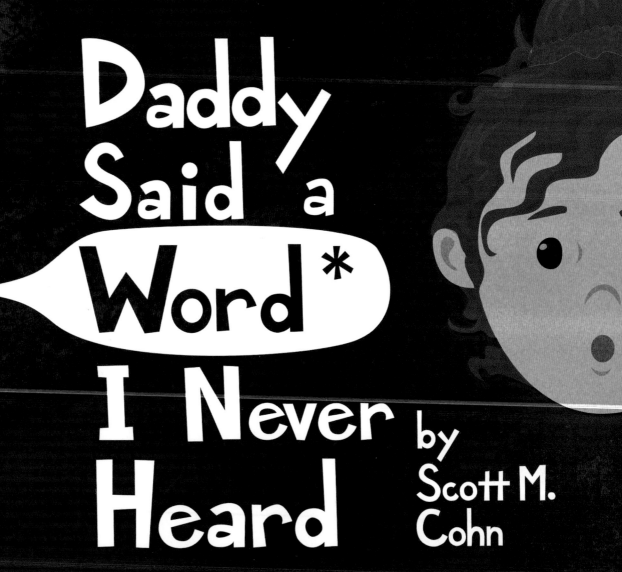

Daddy Said a Word* I Never Heard

by Scott M. Cohn

Ⓛ Ⓑ

Little, Brown and Company

New York   Boston

For my Grandma Bea: just the loveliest person you'll ever meet ♥ —S.M.C.

*Note to reader: The questionable language in this book has been replaced with benign Swedish furniture names.

I was down in the playroom one crisp autumn eve
with Tallulah and Ruby, enjoying some tea.
We'd had a nice portrait made up of us all,
and Daddy was hanging it up on the wall.

He took out a nail from inside his shirt pocket
and, raising his hammer, got ready to sock it.

But apparently things didn't go quite as planned,
and the hammer slammed down with great speed on his hand!

He dropped all his tools
to the floor and turned red.
Then he shouted a word
that I'd never heard said.

Mommy seemed shocked and Daddy got quiet.
I grabbed my best Band-Aid and rushed to apply it.

I bandaged his hand and he put me to bed,
but that word that I'd heard echoed all through my head.

I thought of that time Daddy fell off the pier
and he shouted a word that was new to my ear.

And when Daddy's good buddies came by to play games,
the language they used seemed to be much the same.

And of course every time Uncle Elan stopped by,
I was forced to wear headphones and never told why.

The next day at school we drew turkeys on plates,
but MY turkey looked like a pig on green skates.

I felt very angry and let out a shout,
and that word that I'd heard was the one that came out!

When Mrs. Moran heard my frustrated bleat,
she took me aside and we both had a seat.

She asked where I'd picked up such colorful grammar,
so I told her of Daddy's mistake with the hammer.

She gave me a look that was stern yet sincere.
"We mustn't repeat EVERY word that we hear."

Mrs. Moran said, "Let's put it to rest,"
and the end of the day came without further stress.

At home I found Mommy and Daddy contrite.

I told them, "I think I'd like meat loaf tonight."

It seems that my teacher had called home that day
and asked them to carefully choose what to say.

I thought they'd be mad for what happened at school,
but Daddy came over and pulled up a stool.

"I'm sorry, my sweetie, for filling your head
with those words that your daddy should never have said.
There are still ways of speaking when you get upset
that express how you're feeling and won't cause regret."

"So the next time your drawing just doesn't look right,

or there's not enough wind to go fly your new kite,

you can say, 'I'm not happy' or 'I'm feeling blue,'
then try to find something else fun you can do."

I agreed that the best way to speak, as a rule,
is to use all the good words I'm learning at school.

Peach

Swedish-English Glossary of Furniture

(in order of appearance)

skåp—cabinet

förhänge—drape

fåtölj—easy chair

byrå—bureau

matgrupp—dining room set

spegel—mirror

skohylla—shoe rack

skärbräda—cutting board

sänggavel—headboard

kudde—pillow

hylla—shelf

schäslong—daybed

kylskåp—refrigerator

About This Book

The illustrations for this book were created digitally using Adobe Illustrator and Adobe Photoshop. The text and the display type were set in Daddy.

Copyright © 2015 by Scott M. Cohn • Cover art © 2015 by Scott M. Cohn • Cover design by Scott M. Cohn and Phil Caminiti • Cover copyright © 2015 Hachette Book Group, Inc. • All rights reserved. In accordance with the U.S. Copyright Act of 1976, the scanning, uploading, and electronic sharing of any part of this book without the permission of the publisher is unlawful piracy and theft of the author's intellectual property. If you would like to use material from the book (other than for review purposes), prior written permission must be obtained by contacting the publisher at permissions@hbgusa.com. Thank you for your support of the author's rights. • Little, Brown and Company • Hachette Book Group • 1290 Avenue of the Americas, New York, NY 10104 • Visit us at lb-kids.com • Little, Brown and Company is a division of Hachette Book Group, Inc. • The Little, Brown name and logo are trademarks of Hachette Book Group, Inc. • The publisher is not responsible for websites (or their content) that are not owned by the publisher. • First Edition: November 2015 •Library of Congress Cataloging-in-Publication Data • Cohn. Scott. author. illustrator. • Daddy said a word I've never heard / Scott M. Cohn.-First edition. • pages cm.-(The daddy series : 2) • Summary: At school. a little girl repeats the bad word her father said when he hit his hand with a hammer. so her teacher and parents help her learn that there are better ways to express frustration. • ISBN 978-0-316-40751-9 (hardcover) • [1. Stories in rhyme. 2. Swearing-Fiction. 3. Fathers and daughters-Fiction.] I. Title. II. Title: Daddy said a word I have never heard. • PZ8.3.C6652Dab 2015 • [E]-dc23 • 2014032313 • 10 9 8 7 6 5 4 3 2 1 • SC • Printed in China